Wagons West

Off to Oregon

by Catherine E. Chambers
illustrated by Dick Smolinski

W9-CGW-302

Troll

The sky was bright blue with puffy clouds that looked like the hooped white covers of the wagons. It was April 1854. Jed and Louisa Stoddard were starting the most exciting summer of their lives. They were about to begin the long journey west along the Oregon Trail.

A year ago, Father had died. Then Mother had died of pneumonia a few months later. Jed was fourteen and Louisa only twelve. The State of Virginia thought them too young to be alone. And they had no relatives in Virginia. Their big brother, Jason, had quarreled with Father four years ago and had gone off to the Oregon Territory, far away. The preacher had written to Jason about Father and Mother dying, but no answer came. No one knew if Jason got the letter, or even if Jason himself was still alive. Jed lay awake worrying about being sent to a home for orphans. Then, a month ago, there had been a knock at the door of the house where Jed and Louisa were staying. A tall bearded man in a buckskin suit stood on the porch. It was Jason!

"I've come to take you home to Oregon. I have a farm, and I've just built a house. I'm getting married in the fall!"

3

All at once, sorrow and fear were gone. Jed and Louisa had a family after all! In a week, nearly all the Stoddard household things were sold. "We can't take much with us in a covered wagon," Jason said. Their old house was sold, too. "A share of the money will be for each of us. Some we'll spend on our wagon and supplies," Jason said. "Some I'll keep for you till you're both grown."

At first, Jed and Louisa felt quite shy with Jason. Four years was a long time, and he had changed so much. He used to be what Pa called "wild," and he had always had a temper. Now he worked hard and had patience. And he knew so much about the out-of-doors. "I had to learn" was all Jason would say. "Working your way across the Oregon Trail teaches a person a lot." Jed hoped it would teach him, too. His brother was just the kind of man Jed wanted to become.

Jason had come east from Oregon by the Overland Stage, which could make the trip in only a few weeks. In the wagon train, slow oxen would drag heavy loads. They could cover, at very most, twenty miles a day. That meant two months of travel from Independence—the busy little

Missouri town where the Oregon Trail began—to the Oregon Valley. Then it would take another month or more to reach Jason's farm! Already, Jed, Louisa, and Jason had traveled for a week from their old home to St. Louis. Then they had traveled for a week by steamboat on the Missouri River. They had stayed for several days in Independence, preparing for the rest of their journey.

It seemed to Jed that the whole country had either Oregon Fever or California Fever. That was what folks called the excitement that pulled thousands of people to the gold mines of California or to the fertile fields of the Northwest. Travel across the Great Plains, through Indian country, and across the Rockies could be very hard. People traveled in "trains" of thirty or more wagons, in order to help one another and for protection. These wagon trains formed in Independence.

The days in Independence had been exciting. First, Jason bought a Conestoga wagon. This was the best kind, made in Conestoga, Pennsylvania. Next he bought four strong, patient oxen.

"What shall we name them?" Jed asked eagerly.

Jason grinned. "The ones on the left are called Buck, the ones on the right are called Bright. All ox teams are named that way. Makes it easy for anyone to drive any team if needed." Besides the oxen, they bought a cow named Sukey and a flock of chickens that Louisa would take care of.

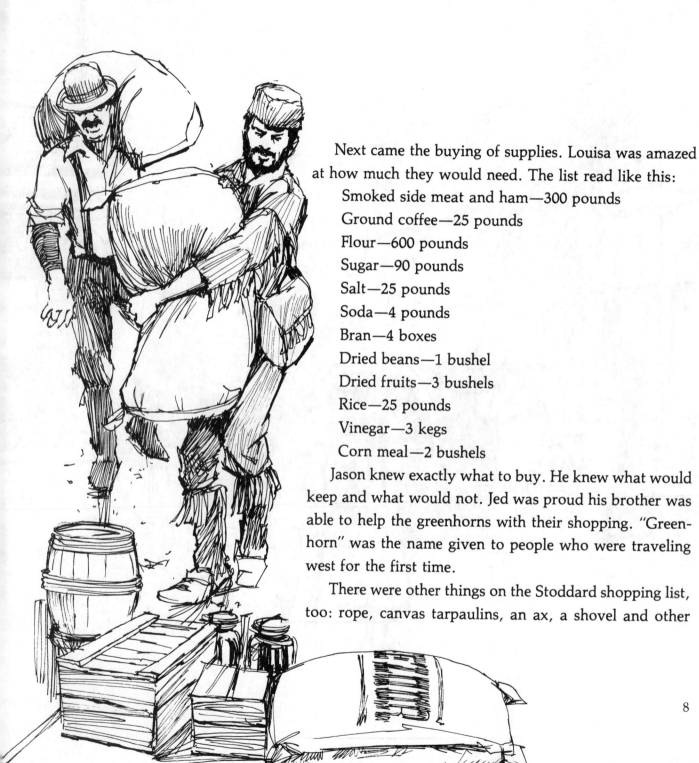

Next came the buying of supplies. Louisa was amazed at how much they would need. The list read like this:

Smoked side meat and ham—300 pounds
Ground coffee—25 pounds
Flour—600 pounds
Sugar—90 pounds
Salt—25 pounds
Soda—4 pounds
Bran—4 boxes
Dried beans—1 bushel
Dried fruits—3 bushels
Rice—25 pounds
Vinegar—3 kegs
Corn meal—2 bushels

Jason knew exactly what to buy. He knew what would keep and what would not. Jed was proud his brother was able to help the greenhorns with their shopping. "Greenhorn" was the name given to people who were traveling west for the first time.

There were other things on the Stoddard shopping list, too: rope, canvas tarpaulins, an ax, a shovel and other

8

tools, a tent, sharp knives, and tin dishes and spoons. They also needed ginger, raisins, and molasses for cooking, plus a water keg. They already had their mother's old iron pot and skillet and her featherbeds and blankets. "Well, that should be everything," Jason told Louisa and Jed.

Other people were buying farm tools and guns and seed potatoes and sheep. Jason helped them with that, too. He already had all that kind of thing in Oregon.

Now it was early morning of the day the trip would begin. The wagons were loaded. The campfires were put out. The night before, around the fires, Jason had been elected captain of the wagon train. He was young, but he was the only man who had made the trip before. Other officers were elected, too. But along the trail, Jason's word would be law.

Jason looked sharply around the camp to make sure that everyone was ready. He cupped his hands. "Off to Oregon!" he called.

"Oregon or bust!" came the reply from the waiting wagons.

Jason rode out in front on his horse, Coyote, and the other officers rode out with him. Four wagons rolled forward, and then four more. This was how they would travel, in four columns. Behind the wagon train came the mules, sheep, and cattle. Dogs ran everywhere, barking with excitement.

The Stoddard wagon was in the third row. Jed's chest swelled as he drove the oxen. Father had taught him how, back on their farm in the Shenandoah Valley. The wagon's canvas side flaps were tied up to let in the early sun. Louisa sat on the wooden board that formed a seat beside Jed, swinging her bare feet. She'd given up shoes as soon as she saw other girls in camp without them. In the next wagon were the Beldersons. Already Harriet Belderson was Louisa's best friend. Jed liked Meg Belderson, who was his own age, and her brother, Tom, who was two years older. Meg was playing her harmonica now. She played a sad, lovely song they had first heard on the riverboat, coming to Independence. Many, many rivers lay ahead. But at the last, the Columbia, their new home was waiting for them!

A week after leaving Independence came their first river crossing. It was the Kaw, or Kansas, River! Excitement crackled through the wagon train. The wagons had to be reformed into a single line and chained together. Every crack in the wagons had to be filled with tar. Guns were hung high up on the wagon frames. Everything was fastened down and wrapped to be watertight. The wagons' canvas covers were drawn so tightly that only small peepholes front and back remained.

Jason rode up beside Jed. "Can you swim? Good. You'd better wade beside the oxen to keep them in line."

Slowly, the wagon train started down the bank into the river. At first, the wagons swayed and jolted. Then they began to sway and rock. They were floating. The oxen were swimming. Jed was swimming, too. All at once the current began to push against them. The wagon tipped badly and banged against one of the oxen. Jed tried to steer the wagon back and couldn't.

Louisa's face appeared. "I'm coming to help."

"Get back!" Jed shouted. "It's too dangerous!"

"I can swim! You taught me!" Louisa slid into the river, her dress ballooning around her. She helped hold the wagon straight. Behind them, Tom and Meg Belderson were doing the same thing. It seemed a very long time before the noise of the water turned into the sucking of mud against the oxen's hoofs. They were on land again.

Everyone was glad to set up camp that night!

The days on the trail fell into a pattern. At four o'clock in the morning, Jason fired three shots from his rifle. Sleepily, people began climbing from the wagons. Everyone had a job to do. Some people rounded up the oxen. Some unchained the wagons. Some took down the tents. Children gathered fuel and stoked up fires. Women began cooking sowbelly, or bacon, and special pancakes called slam-johns. Soon delicious smells rose with the smoke of the fires. Bean pots, which had been buried to bake overnight, were dug up. Kettles were scoured. Water kegs were filled. Oxen were yoked to wagons. Everyone was in place, ready and waiting when the bugle sounded at 7:00 A.M. By now the sky had turned from gray to pale pink and yellow to clear blue.

The four wagons that led the way yesterday took the rear today. The lead positions changed every day. That way everyone took a turn at riding through the cloud of dust in the rear of the wagon train.

In the morning the men drove the wagons. Often Jason and a few other men on horses rode ahead to hunt. There were antelope on the plains and prairie chicken. When they reached the banks of the South Platte River, a cry rang out from wagon to wagon. *"Buffalo!"*

There they were, just as in the pictures Jed had seen. Thousands of shaggy brown beasts lumbering over the hills of sand. The sound of their hoofs roared like thunder and the ground shook beneath them.

All at once a slim figure flashed like silver among the buffalo. It was Jason on his horse, Coyote! Jed's heart pounded like a hammer. But Jason and Coyote knew what they were doing. Coyote was a good buffalo horse. He darted this way and that, dodging the buffalo bulls. He knew how to put Jason in position for the best shot. Jason was a good buffalo hunter, too. He shot three buffalo in the only proper place, just behind the right shoulder. Rifle balls wouldn't go through the matted hair and thick bone of a buffalo's head. That day, when the wagon train stopped for "nooning," there was fresh buffalo meat to eat.

Nooning was the midday stop all wagons made to rest the animals during the noontime heat. The animals drank and rested in the shade of the wagons. Usually the oxen stayed yoked, because in an hour they would be on the way again.

In the afternoon everyone was tired. The wagons moved more slowly. Women and boys drove the wagons now, while the men napped. Louisa was the lady of the Stoddard wagon—she not only drove in the afternoon,

16

she cooked the meals. They weren't bad, either, Jed had to admit. It was Jason who showed her how to make prairie-chicken stew spiced with sage leaves. Jason also taught the greenhorns how to roast buffalo ribs and how to boil buffalo tongue. "Indians and mountain men think that's the best part of a buffalo. I've seen them leave all the rest of the meat for wolves and coyotes." The members of the wagon train cut the buffalo meat into strips and dried them in the sun.

In late afternoon Jason and a few young men rode ahead to pick a campsite. Jason marked a circle for the wagon train to form when it arrived. He had to make this just the right size. Too small, and all the wagons would not fit around it. Too large, and there would be gaps between the wagons that Indians or wild animals could break through. After a week Jason could make his circles exactly the right size. While he did this, the other young men dug water holes.

Soon the wagon train arrived. Again, everyone had a job to do. Wagons were driven into place and chained together for the night. The oxen were turned loose to graze. Horses and mules were tied up so they could not wander. Children scattered to gather fuel for the fires—dried grasses or wood, if there was any. Women brought out their tinderboxes. Striking a spark with flint and steel could be hard work. Whoever got a flame going first shared her "fire" with the others. Once the fires were lit, the smell of cooking filled the air.

After supper, dishes and kettles were scoured with sand. Bean pots were buried next to the fires. Then there was dancing and singing, gossiping and bragging. Meg Belderson brought out her harmonica. A man in one of the other wagons played a fiddle. The songs rose up into the darkening sky.

Later, fires were banked, or covered with ashes, to keep them burning low for the night, and the camp settled to sleep. Every night Jason picked a different man to stand guard with a rifle. People slept in wagons, in tents, or on the ground. Jed liked to lie on his back on the earth,

between campfire and wagon, and look up at the bright stars. Sometimes he heard the far-off lonely howling of coyotes.

When the rains came, camping wasn't as much fun. Rain leaked through the wagon cover no matter what Jed did. Louisa couldn't keep a fire going. They ate cold dried meat and soggy biscuits, as they huddled together in the damp. One night, in the middle of blackness, a clap of thunder split the sky. The men grabbed their guns, thinking it was an Indian attack. Then lightning crackled, and the rain poured down. They ran for their wagons. Animals were screaming with fear. Louisa was shaking all over. Jed wrapped blankets around her. He pulled the wagon cover as tightly shut as he could. Through the opening he watched the lightning. Even while he was scared he knew how beautiful it was.

19

Make camp, break camp, follow the river. Everywhere they went, there were rivers. They crossed the South Platte, which was swift and dangerous. Mules dug in their heels and brayed with fear. "They must know about the quicksand," Jason said. Then the wagons followed the north fork of the Platte River. Past Court House Rock, past Chimney Rock poking its finger straight up into the sky. Past Scotts Bluff with its strange house-shapes jutting up in cliffs. The country here was wild and beautiful. There were no trees, except the cottonwoods along the river. The land by the river was flat and green with prairie grass. Beyond rose the rocks, suddenly a thousand feet high, as though carved by a long-gone giant. The rocks were strange and wonderful colors, like the sky, and they seemed to shimmer in the noontime heat.

Day after day, the wagon train followed the Platte. "A thousand miles long, a mile wide, an inch deep, and all of it muddy!" Mr. Belderson joked. A month and a half after they left Independence, Fort Laramie loomed ahead. In the wagons, everyone perked up. Young ladies began to wipe the dust from their faces. Fort Laramie was a U.S. Army camp, bought from the American Fur Company. It was built of dried mud bricks, and its two blockhouses had slits through which guns could be fired.

"They're not used much now," Jason told Jed and Louisa. "The Indians around here are friendly with the settlers." Jed had been wondering when he was going to see Indians.

Fort Laramie

There were many at the Fort, trading buffalo robes and other wares. They looked fearsome with their braids and feathers and scarred faces. The wagon train rested at Laramie for two days. It felt good not to be jostled every minute with the movement of the jolting wagons. The soldiers held a dance in the stockade the first night, and the next night the soldiers were guests of the pioneers around the campfires. On the third day, Jason's bugle-call sounded at dawn.

The hills became mountains now. Snow-covered peaks loomed on either side. They passed Independence Rock, where hundreds of earlier pioneers had carved their names. Jed added his with Jason's knife. They came to the bleak, steep gorge of the Devil's Gate. They followed the Sweetwater River. It was midsummer, and they had been on the trail two months.

Often it was hard for the oxen to pick their way up the steep, narrow path. Only the old and sick rode in the wagons now. The others walked to lighten the load. Some families had to leave behind heavy things that they had

brought. Jed and Louisa saw chests, chairs, and plows that earlier travelers had left behind.

"How much farther to Oregon?" Jed kept asking.

At last, Jason grinned tiredly. "We'll get to the top of the Elephant's Back in a day or so."

Jed felt a thrill of excitement. "The top of the Elephant's Back" meant the Continental Divide. All rivers on one side flowed east to the Atlantic. All rivers on the other side flowed west to the Pacific. That night Mr. Belderson teased everyone about how very hard it would be to get the wagons through a mountain pass. Jason whispered to Jed that the pass was so easy Mr. Belderson probably wouldn't know when he reached it.

They kept traveling upward. Just before noon the next day they came out suddenly into a broad green valley. On each side were small green hills. Beyond them, above them rose the mountain peaks . . . tree-covered, snow-covered, dazzling in the sun. Midway into the valley, Jason fired a shot.

"Welcome to Oregon Territory!" he cried.

They had another week of travel through sharp cliffs. Then they were near Fort Bridger. This was the trading post started by the famous mountain man Jim Bridger. "I met him on my first trip out," Jason told Louisa and Jed that night beside the fire. "He's one of the greatest of the mountain men. He's been a trapper since he was your age. He's been an Army scout. He discovered the Great Salt Lake. I wish you could see him! He's probably out guiding a wagon train himself."

When they rolled into Fort Bridger the next day, a granite-faced man in a flat-brimmed hat came out to meet them. Jason let out a cry. "Jim! Old Jim Bridger!" Jed shook hands with Jason's idol.

After Fort Bridger came the worst part of the trip. Hot, dry July days under a burning sun. More steep, narrow paths. More treasures brought from home were discarded. No grass, no game. Children loved the fizzing water of Soda Springs, and the sound like the *chuff* of steamboats at Steamboat Springs. But the water was not good to drink. Some animals died of heat and thirst.

"This land looks like the way the moon must be," Jed said to Meg Belderson as they trudged along. Meg nodded without speaking. Her black hair clung damply to her tanned face. Louisa, too, was browned and had calluses on her feet.

25

They reached Fort Boise, the Hudson's Bay Company
trading post on the Snake River. They followed the Burnt
River valley and turned north—past Lone Pine Tree
Mountain, into the Grande Ronde valley, then into the
Blue Mountains. They were catching salmon now for their

evening meals. It was fun to stand in the rushing water and scoop up the leaping fish with their hands.

The nights came sooner. It was mid-August now. The once-white wagon covers were torn and dirty. Some wagons had broken on the mountain trails. They had been rebuilt as carts. The oxen were tired and thin from the long travel. Their necks were sore from the yokes, and some of them limped. Even though days were shorter, it sometimes seemed to Jed that they would never end. He often thought he couldn't drive a wagon, haul water, or yoke the oxen one more time. But then one day, they came to the Columbia River and turned west along it into the Willamette Valley.

The ground was no longer parched and dry. It was green. Leafy trees lifted tall branches above log houses. Wheat and corn waved their golden heads. People came from the houses to greet the travelers with fresh vegetables and cool milk. Everyone was talking about how fine the farmland was here, and how warm the winters. Each day, one or two families would drop out of the wagon train to stake out land for farms.

One night Jed came back to the wagon to find Jason looking at himself in a tin plate. He was trimming his beard. At first, Jed thought Jason had gone crazy. Then he started to grin.

"We're almost home!"

"Tomorrow! You and Louisa will see your new house and my bride-to-be! She's taking care of the place while I'm away."

In midmorning Jason tooted a joyful song on the bugle. The whole wagon train ground to a halt. Jason stood in his stirrups and turned to the others. "This is good-bye for the Stoddards. I've been proud to be your captain this far. You can make it on your own now. Just keep heading west, and you'll reach the ocean! Remember where we live, and come back to visit!"

Mr. Belderson looked around. "Seems to me you've picked a fine place. Any land left here for some more neighbors?"

"Sure," Jason said. He clapped Mr. Belderson on the back. Then he whirled Coyote and galloped off across the valley. The Stoddard and Belderson wagons rolled gaily after.

They came to well-kept fields. They came to a
sprawling log house under leafy trees. A young woman
with bright black eyes was walking from the barn carrying
a basket. She stopped and stared, and then she started to
run.

Jason galloped to meet her, swung her up, and kissed
her. Then he turned to the others, his face bright as the
sun. "Louisa, Jed—say hello to Caroline. And welcome
home!"

Index

*(Page numbers that appear in **boldface** type refer to illustrations.)*

Copyright © 1984 by Troll Communications L.L.C.

All rights reserved. No part of this book may be reproduced or
utilized in any form or by any means, electronic or mechanical,
including photocopying, recording, or by any information storage
and retrieval system, without written permission from the publisher.

This edition published 2000 by Troll Communications L.L.C.

Printed in the United States of America.

10   9   8   7   6   5   4   3   2   1

Cover art by Robert F. Goetzl.

Library of Congress Cataloging-in-Publication Data

Chambers, Catherine E.
    Wagons West.

    (Adventures in frontier America)
    Summary: Two children travel with their older brother
across the country by wagon train from Virginia to
the Oregon Territory.
    [1. Overland journeys to the Pacific—Fiction.
2. Frontier and pioneer life—Fiction.   I. Smolinski,
Dick, ill.   II. Title.   III. Series: Chambers,
Catherine E. Adventures in frontier America.
PZ7.C3558Wag   1984   [Fic]   83-18276
    ISBN 0-8167-0043-5 (lib. bdg.)
    ISBN 0-8167-6294-5 (pbk.)